The
Growing Story

By Ruth Krauss

Illustrated by
Helen Oxenbury

HarperCollins *Publishers*

The Growing Story
Text copyright © 1947, 1975 by Ruth Krauss
Illustrations copyright © 2007 by Helen Oxenbury
Manufactured in China.

Library of Congress Cataloging-in-Publication Data
Krauss, Ruth.
The growing story / by Ruth Krauss / illustrated by Helen Oxenbury.
— Newly illustrated ed.   p. cm.
Summary: A little boy worries throughout the summer that he's not getting bigger,
but at the end of the season he tries on his winter clothes and realizes that he has grown.
ISBN-10: 0-06-024716-9 (trade bdg.) — ISBN-13: 978-0-06-024716-4 (trade bdg.)
ISBN-10: 0-06-024717-7 (lib. bdg.) — ISBN-13: 978-0-06-024717-1 (lib. bdg.)
[1. Growth—Fiction.] I. Oxenbury, Helen, ill. II. Title.
PZ7.K875 Gt 2007   97-42822   [E]—dc21

Typography by Carla Weise
3 4 5 6 7 8 9 10
❖
Newly Illustrated Edition

For Tom

—H.O.

A boy and a puppy and some
chicks were all very little.

Summer was coming. Buds grew
on the trees. The grass began to grow.
On the side of the barn, flowers began
to grow.

The little boy said to his mother,
"Everything is growing. The grass
is growing. The flowers are
growing. The trees
are growing."

He asked her, "Will the chicks grow?"
"Of course," his mother replied.
He asked her, "Will the puppy grow?"
"Of course," his mother replied.
He asked her, "Will I grow too?"
"Of course you'll grow too,"
his mother replied.

The days grew longer. The nights grew shorter.
The grass grew faster. The flowers grew higher.
Leaves grew big on the trees.

The little boy said to the puppy and the chicks,
"We're growing too."

The air was growing warmer. The little boy and his mother planted corn seeds in the field.

His mother said, "We'll put away your warm woolen clothes. When summer is over you'll put them on again."

They folded up his warm pants
and put them away in a box. They
folded up his warm coat and put it
away in the box.

The little boy climbed on a chair
and put the box on a shelf.

The corn grew. Blossoms grew on the orchard
trees. Lilacs bloomed by the barn.
The chicks grew taller. The puppy grew taller.
The little boy said, "You both grew taller."

He said to his mother, "They both grew taller.
I don't feel taller."
He asked her, "Am I growing too?"
"Oh yes. Of course," his mother replied.

Little pears grew on the orchard trees. Little ears grew on the corn. The grass grew still faster.

The chicks grew still taller. The puppy grew still taller. The little boy looked in a looking-glass. He said to his mother, "The chicks have grown taller than my knee. The puppy has grown taller than my middle. I don't look taller."

He asked her, "Are you sure I am growing?"

His mother replied, "Of course you are growing."

The honeysuckle bloomed. The roses bloomed.
The corn grew as high as a man. The pears were ripening.
   The chicks grew still taller again. The puppy grew
still taller again.
   The little boy went alone and sat by the side of the
barn. He looked at the grass and the flowers. He looked

at the trees and the corn. He looked at the puppy
and looked at the chicks.

He said, "Everything is still growing. I can see
they are growing."

He asked, "Can I really be growing too?"

Summer was growing to its end.

The ripe pears fell. The days grew shorter. The nights grew longer again. The grass grew slower again.

When the leaves grew red and yellow and
brown, summer was over. The corn was over.
No flowers bloomed on the side of the barn.
The chicks had grown up. The chicks were
chickens. The chickens were nearly up to the
little boy's middle.

The puppy had grown up. The puppy was
a dog. The dog was nearly up to the little boy's
head.

The little boy looked at the chickens and the
dog. "You both have grown up. I haven't grown
up. I am still little," the little boy said.

The air had grown colder. The little boy's mother said, "We'll take out your warm woolen clothes and put them on again."

The little boy climbed on the chair and took down the box from the shelf. They took out his warm pants from the box and unfolded them. They took out his warm coat from the box and unfolded it.

The little boy put on his warm pants again and looked in the looking-glass. "My pants are too tight. The legs are too short," he said.

He put on the warm coat again and looked
in the looking-glass. "My coat is too tight.
The sleeves are too short," he said.

He put on his cap and ran out into the yard. He turned a somersault. He threw his cap in the air.

"Hey!" the little boy said to the chickens and the dog. "My pants are too little and my coat is too little.

"I'm
growing
too."